REMUDA DUST

By Fred Engel

Published by
Benchmark Publishing, Inc., Park City, Utah, U.S.A.

ISBN 0-9637705-2-7

Typeset by The Village Scribe, Park City, Utah
For information, contact:
Benchmark Publishing, Inc.
Park City, Utah
(801) 647-9202

CONTENTS

DEDICATION

To

All My Family

And

Friends

For the Encouragement and Support

I Received From Them.

ACKNOWLEDGMENTS

I have been supported by many people in
developing this book of poetry.
In particular, I would like to acknowledge those
people who have produced the paintings and
photographs, that help make this book what it is.

Western Paintings by:

Tim Cox
P.O. Box 637
Eagle Creek
Clifton, AZ 85533
(505) 538-5376 (#6002)

Photographs by:

Kay Wooster Anderson
Novato, California
(415) 883-4219

and

Linda York
Scotts Valley, California

ABOUT THE AUTHOR

Putting my thoughts down on paper with my pen, has been an attempt on my part to preserve some of the experiences or feelings I've had, and has allowed me at times, to savor somethings that otherwise would have become maybe just a faint memory. My perspective comes from my own observations and my personal real life experiences. Somethings I've written have come to me while on horseback working cattle, or while driving a truck. Other things have come from just every day living. I don't claim to be an old time cowboy, but my way of life is "the cowboy way".

My purpose for printing this small collection of some of my favorite things I've written down, is a hope that it will bring you enjoyment and maybe remind you of somethings that we never want to be lost.

I hope you'll find that from time to time you'll be able to pick this book up and turn to some pages that you'll be able to read over and over, and find enjoyment, each time you read them.

Fred Engel
Corralitos, California

INTRODUCTION

The Remuda is a name used by the cowboys when referring to their horses that are being used as replacement mounts. A cowboy will usually rotate the horses he uses on a daily basis so he'll be somewhat assured of having a fresh mount at the beginning of each day (although he may not be too fresh himself).

These extra horses are usually allowed to tag along loose and will generally stay in a little herd of their own; hence "The Remuda". Obviously, then, the dust they make can be called Remuda Dust. As it settles it becomes one of the ingredients to make up the cowboy flavor of things.

That's what this little collection of things I've scribbled down from time to time is supposed to do... just kind of give a cowboy flavor to things.

I'M A COWBOY

I'm a cowboy and proud of it
And maybe part of a dying breed,
But it seems to be the place I fit
And it gives me what I need.

As I watch the sun rise above the hill,
At the break of a brand new day,
I catch my horse, startle some quail,
Just stand there and watch 'em fly away.
Then I tack up my patient horse,
And head out for my day's work.
I lean in the saddle, making sure it's tight,
Jus' ride away 'n spit into the dirt.

'Cause, I'm a cowboy and proud of it,
And maybe part of a dying breed,
But it seems to be the place I fit
And it gives me what I need.

And as I ride along this barb wire fence
Stretchin' it straight and tight with my two hands,
I trod through a sea of wild oats,
A golden ocean covering the land.
And I can see a white face cow
With her newborn calf's head
Pressed against her side.

And I'm glad to be a cowboy
As I sit on top this horse that I ride.

Yes, I'm a cowboy and proud of it,
And maybe part of a dying breed,
But it seems to be the place I fit
And it gives me what I need.

MOVIN' THE REMUDA

We were moving the Remuda
Just upstream aways
And it was one of those picturesque
Cowboy kind of days.
The horses were snortin' and splashed
As they ran
And we hazed 'em with our loops
That we swung in our hands.
The air was filled with the smell
Of things that were wet
Including us, leather, horse hide
And sweat.
We were headed towards new grass
Where the horses could feed,
And this big cranky gelding
Was takin' the lead.
The rest followed but didn't know
That he knew
That just up the stream
Was where that tall grass grew.

5   *Remuda Dust*

THE GRAND ENTRY

They enter the arena one by one,
Proud, strong, but controlled,
Are the horses that run.
And the colors are presented at a rodeo or fair,
By pretty gals wearing hats,
But, with wind in their hair.
And the announcer speaks,
With a tone in his voice,
That says he's a cowboy too,
And that it's by choice.
And as he announces each flag,
And tells what it means,
It's one of the most stirring sights
That can be seen.
The thrill of seeing the flags as they fly,
And the excitement in the crowd
As the horses run by,
Gives a feeling to most, you can't explain inside,
And puts a lump in your throat,
And makes you swell with pride.

TEAM PENNING

When cuttin' cattle out of the herd,
Go slow and easy, it's much preferred.
Keep 'em bunched up, and keep 'em quiet,
It's better that way, no need for a riot.
Now working 'em out one by one,
Is the best way to go to get the job done.
Then drive 'em away from all the rest,
And pen 'em all up, and do your best
To keep 'em from goin' straight back to the herd,
'Cause you're looking for a first,
Not a last or a third!
Now team penning is what I'm talkin' about,
When you're looking for your numbers
And cutting 'em out.
But I've seen those, at the county fair,
While racing the clock,
And in the excitement there,
Hit that herd like a cue ball that breaks
The billiards on the table,
In a game of high stakes.
And when the cattle scatter, they're lucky to find
Even one head to pen,
Before running out of time.
And then there's the cattle that stick to the fence
Or just lay right down during these events,
And just won't move, no matter what you do,
'Til you hear,

"No more time gang, you're all through".
But the crowd still cheers and claps their hands,
And you're glad you're out there,
And not sitting in the stands.

9   *Remuda Dust*

THE HIGH DESERT PLAIN

Early in the fall on the high desert plain,
Or maybe just after a late summer rain,
When the sky turns pink,
And the hills deepen their hue,
And we're doing the things that us cowboys do,
Like gathering cattle or sortin' out pairs,
And there's that cowboy feeling,
Just hangin' in the air,
I'll take time to think of how it might be
If the Lord hadn't given this way of life to me.
Would I know the smell of a storm blowin' in,
Or feel the change of the seasons,
That ride on the wind?
Would I know the scent,
Of the sagebrush in bloom,
And would I know how
To weather a range monsoon?
And as I continue to ponder,
What I do and don't know
I think of the Cheyenne, and the Sioux,
And the buffalo,
And how this land was once theirs to roam,
And how now I find comfort being out here
Alone.

THE RAIN

It started rainin' out here today,
I wonder how long this rain will stay.
It's been for us a long dry spell,
The pastures are all brown
And no water'n the well.
The dust's drunk up every single drop
As it's come down.
Then at a trot,
I head for cover to the nearest tree.
It's been a while since it's fallen on me.
Water's been rationed, the amount we can use,
Hope this here storm's a sign of good news.
I can remember the rain, when I was a kid,
And remember how it smelled,
And the things I did.
And it seems my mom
Would always be there to say,
"Stay inside now, you can't go out today."
But I was a kid and liked mud 'tween my toes,
And could care less about a cold in my nose.
And I remember how, when it really came down,
How it would hit the roof,
And how it would sound.
And I could smell it comin' from miles away,
As it dampened the dirt and fell on the hay.

13   *Remuda Dust*

THERE'S SOMETHING ABOUT IT

Have you ever heard a rooster crow,
As down the road you did go,
On your way to the corner store?
There's something about it.
I can't live without it.
I've got to hear that rooster crow once more.

Have you ever smelled tall grass that grows,
In a field 'long side a country road,
And heard the meadow lark sing its song?
There's something about it.
I can't live without it.
The country is the place where I belong.

Has mud oozed up between your toes,
As you watched the water as it flows,
On its way to irrigate a field?
There's something about it.
I can't live without it.
I love the country and I always will.

Have you ever been where the only sound,
Is a tractor plowin' up the ground,
Or taken a nap in the shade of a big ol' tree?
There's something about it.
I can't live without it.
The country's got to be the place for me.

Have you ever been sittin' in the saddle,
On a good horse while workin' cattle,
With your hat pulled down,
And sweat dripping down your brow?
There's something about it.
I can't live without it.
I thank the Lord he made a horse and cow.

Have you ever rolled on down the road,
Pulling 20 tons of payload,
For 3,000 miles until you get back home?
There's something about it.
You'll talk all about it.
If you're ever out there on the road alone.

Have you ever smelled new mowed hay,
In the freshness of a brand new day,
Or awakened to a gentle summer rain?
There's something about it.
I can't live without it.
There's nothing you'll ever know,
That's quite the same.

Have you ever felt the warm night air,
In the evening, on the porch, in that chair,
That's no longer kept in the house?
There's something about it.
There's no doubt about it.
You can sit out there 'til all the lights are out.

Do you know the fragrance in the air,
Late at night at the county fair,
From the back of a pickup truck,
On your way home?
There's something about it,
You never will forget it,
When you're not in that pickup all alone!

COWBOY STYLE

To sound like a cowboy is an art in itself
To make the right words
Just spill out of your mouth.
You got to be colorful
And use an expression or two
If you want to sound like most cowboys do.
You should change a few words, just a little,
And put on a different ending,
Or stretch out the middle.
Maybe use a wrong word that sounds almost right
And say things like,
"Grab holt a this" not "hold on tight".
And when talking 'bout horses
And how good you can ride,
Let 'em know you can "fork a bronc" but don't
Tack on too much brag.
And if a rodeo cowboy was ever heard to say
"Pinto" for "paint" or "dark brown" for "bay"
When referring to the luck of his draw that day,
It might be grounds when heard,
Jawing like that,
To withdraw his buckle, spurs, boots and hat.
Now if you've got to go somewhere and really
Must leave,
Here's a couple more sayings you can put up
Your sleeve.

"I gotta eat up some asphalt"
Or, "Grab some gone"
Or "I'm burning up daylight and can't stay long"
And when cowboys talk, there ain't no mistakes,
They don't speak English,
They talk United States.

THE MEETIN' AT THE DANCE

Well, I's at this dance hall, at this here dance,
When out o' the corner of my eye,
I hap'd to glance
At this good lookin' gal,
In these nice fittin' pants.
I thought to myself, she must be new in town,
'Cause I hadn't seen her before, hangin' around.
Now I didn't have to think about
It too much more,
Before I decided I was gonna ask her
Out on that floor.
So I tipped back my hat and made sure
My collar's straight,
And started walkin' toward her,
But I's a little too late!
'Cause about that same time, some other guy
Went on up to her and kindly said "Hi".
Well, they strolled out there together,
And started to dance
While I just stood there in silence,
Still admiring those pants.
Well, it seemed like the band
Was never gonna quit,
And that I'd better find someone else
With a good lookin' fit.
I watched them dance and saw,
That they's having their fun,

So I thought, well, I'd better forget it,
And move on along.
But then the band announced that
They's takin' a break,
And I saw that what I'd been thinkin'
Might be a mistake.
'Cause this guy that had first asked her to dance
Just walked away, and it gave me the chance,
To try again and see if she would
Join me out there, on that ol' hard wood.
So I went on over and I said "Hi.",
And "Would you like to dance with me, or, are
You with that other guy?"
Well, she accepted and we began to talk,
And I's happy that other guy had taken a walk.
We danced a few dances,
Out there with each other,
And I's glad I hadn't give up and asked another.
But she said she had to leave tho'
It was still kind of early,
And I thought if I wanted to act,
I'd have to hurry.
So I asked if she's comin'
To this dance next week,
And if so, could she put up again
With my two left feet?

She said, Well, we'll see", then said goodbye,
And disappeared out the door,
With that other guy.
Now the next week at the dance, she didn't show,
So I figured I hadn't impressed her,
Don't you know.
But all wasn't lost, because you see,
Before she left that night, she'd given to me
Her phone number.
So I thought I'd call,
And find out why she hadn't shown up that night
At the hall.
She told me that tho' she'd wanted to go
She hadn't felt all that good and had been movin'
Quite slow.
But that she felt better now,
And thanks for the call,
And that maybe this week,
She'd return to the hall.
Well, we talked a little before saying goodbye,
But I still kind of wondered about that other guy.
Now when the next week rolled around to the
Night of the dance,
I was lookin' again for those nice fittin' pants.
But when I walked on in, I didn't see her at first,
So I bought me a beer just to quench my thirst.
And as I stood there takin' a big ol' swaller,
She went waltzin' on by, with that other feller.

So I thought what the heck, and started to dance,
With someone else, then I gave her a glance,
And tipped my hat while two-steppin' by,
Makin' sure she'd see me, tryin' to say hi.
Well, when the music quit, I went on over
And she said, "Hi, this is my sister-in-law,
And this guy here, well he's my brother".
Somewhat relieved and with a hidden sigh,
I'd finally found out now, about that other guy.
Her brother? I thought, well what a surprise!
Well, we danced together,
And after breakin' the ice,
I asked her for a date,
And she thought it was nice.
So we went out to dinner,
To get to know one another,
And we went out alone,
We didn't take her brother!

REMUDA DUST

Following the Remuda while eatin' their dust,
I was thinking about the wranglers,
And what about us.
We work all day long with these cattle too,
But we don't get days off like these horses do.
You know with a few days on,
And a few days off,
Having a job like ours wouldn't be that tough.
So I thought extra hands ought to be hired,
For a "cowboy remuda" so we wouldn't get tired.
But then I thought again and came to agree,
That maybe a cowboy remuda,
Wouldn't be for me.
'Cause I'd hate to find out it was time for work,
By feeling a rope on my neck and havin' it jerk.
And I'd rather be tired,
The more I gave it some thought,
Than packin' tack and chewin' on a bit.
So I'll just do my job and be tired if I must
'Cause it's not all that bad, eatin' Remuda dust.

Remuda Dust 24

THE RIDE

Back in my youth one summer day,
I took a little ride on my 6 year old bay.
We went through the pasture,
And out past the grove,
And across the ravine to the neighbors dirt road.
We followed it south for about a mile,
And trailin' along was my old dog Pal.
Now Pal was just a mutt,
But a good dog, you see,
And I could always count on him being with me.
We'd go places we thought no one had been,
And play Cowboys and Indians, just me and him.
And one day while exploring
The Wild West frontier,
We went to a place not too far from here.
There was nothing built out there
At the time we went,
No buildings of any kind,
It was good times we spent.
It was just rolling hills and oats had been sown
Earlier in the year and were not yet full grown.
They hadn't been cut or raked or baled.
And if we'd had a boat we might have sailed
Off to the horizon, 'cause as far as we could see
It looked like ocean currents to old Pal and me.
Well now it's all changed and all built up,

With roads that are paved,
And buildings and such,
But I'll always remember how it was that day,
When I rode out there with Pal
On my 6 year old bay.

ROPE BURNS AND FROSTBITE

At times it may seem senseless,
As to what goes on in life.
It may seem you're faced with anger,
Maybe pain and sometimes strife.
And it may not always work out
The way you think things ought to be.
But you're not out there all alone,
It's like that for everyone, including you and me.
Try and take the things that happen,
And take them all in stride,
Because the worst thing to happen,
Would be to lose your confidence or self pride.
Now take the old time cowboy,
And look at his way of life,
Filled with sweat, and dirt, and leather,
A plate of beans, rope burns and frostbite.
His ways are viewed by many,
As romantic, glamorous and free.
And his ways are usually envied,
By folks like you and me.
But I think what we envy,
And what we like to feel inside,
Is the cowboy's confidence, determination,
And his sense of self-pride.

Remuda Dust 28

BILLY THE STRAY

He wandered into our camp one day,
Not long after he'd just run away.
He was tired and alone and hungry, I'd say,
Just a pitiful lookin' little ol' stray.
His clothes were worn thin, and dirty to boot,
And he wore no socks, 'cause he had no shoes.
His pony was thin and worn out too,
And he looked kinda sad when he looked at you.
He asked "Who's the ramrod here, 'cause I'm
Looking for work?"
And you could tell by lookin' that he was tired,
And full of hurt.
Then the boss said "What's your name, son,
And what can you do?
And give me a good reason,
Why I should hire you."
He said "my real name's William,
But I'm never called that.
Most folks call me Billy, and I'm used to it.
I know some about horses and can throw a rope.
And if I'm hired on with you boys,
I'll be a good cowpoke."
So the boss said "O.K. Billy, I'll let you stay.
But the work is hard and makes a long day.
So pull your own weight and earn your pay.
'Less you'd rather remain just a little ol' stray.

You can start by helping Cookie,
And gather him some wood.
Then help round up the horses,
If you think you could."
And with that job description, if you will,
The boss hired on our young stray Bill.
And as days went on we all taught him things
And found him some old boots,
And a pair of old jeans.
We taught him to load the wagon,
And to hitch up the team,
And we had him sort all the rocks,
Out of the beans.
And we taught him things that should be known
By all young cowboys not yet fully grown.
We taught him to rope and to dally up tight
When his loop caught steer that was full of fight.
And when the cattle got spooked,
And need quieted down,
We'd call Billy to help since we had him around.
And he still makes his livin' by chasin' a cow,
And he's been with us, I guess,
'Bout 20 years now.

31   *Remuda Dust*

A COLD DECEMBER MORNING

On a cold December morning,
Miles and miles from town,
I was way up in the mountains,
And snow was on the ground.
The coals were still hot
From my fire last night,
So I stoked them a little
'Til a new flame shown bright.
Then I pulled from my pack
Some supplies I'd brought
And made some coffee and bacon,
It was good and was hot.
I grained my horses,
And packed up my camp,
And brushed off the snow,
So things wouldn't get damp.
Then with my hat on my head
And my coat buttoned tight,
I rode down the mountain
And was home before night.

BUCKIN' HAY

I was buckin' hay, one summer day.
I had to work but wanted to play,
Is what I do, worth the pay?
I really rather had stayed home that day.
Dilemmas like this being common to me
I wondered if I'd always be
Sittin' up on some load o' hay
Wonderin'... should I work, or should I play?
Now buckin' hay in that ol' hot sun
You know for sure ain't too much fun.
The more I work, the more I sweat,
But the less I work the more I'm in debt.
Sometimes it seems I just can't win,
But it seems to be the fix I'm in.
Cut and rake and bale the hay,
Then load and stack it high to stay,
Out in the field until the day,
I load it again for not much pay,
On the truck and stack it high.
And once again I have to sigh,
Feelin' every muscle begin to ache,
Some days I think my back will break.
But in the words of my grandpa
And rememberin' about him and what I saw,
"Whatever your job, do it well,
It'll keep you, boy, from going to hell".

He'd always do the best he could,
Whether it was plowin' ground or stackin' wood.
Then he'd usually say with a half way grin
"Early to bed, early to rise
Makes a man healthy"...
He'd leave off the "wealthy and wise",
And I seemed to know just what he meant
Knowing he'd worked hard for each red cent.
So wantin' to be as good as him,
I just let that sweat roll off my brim.

PUPPIES - THE WARNING

If you stop at the feed store
On your way to town,
And you spot a box full of puppies
Just sittin' on the ground,
Be careful not to pet them
And whatever you do,
Don't look 'em in the eye,
When they look back at you.
'Cause it happened to me
On my way to town,
When I picked one up
That I couldn't put down.
I didn't see 'em right off
but then heard 'em cry,
And thought, well, I'll just look
Then pass 'em on by.
But right then and there was my big undoing
And I think it was just about two days
Before he started his chewin'.
At the time I didn't think,
What the matter would be
If I'd just pick one up,
And take him home with me.
'Cause dogs are considered to be
Man's best friend,
Since he's a good companion
And all that, to him.

He can help with your cattle,
And take care of your sheep,
And give you protection at night when you sleep.
But for puppies the above is not always true,
Because all they do is eat, poop and chew.

CASH IN ADVANCE

So you're all out of money
And way down on your luck.
And the gas gauge is past empty,
In your old pick-up truck.
And your bills are piling up,
And all way past due,
And the bill collectors are callin' on you?
Well, you can try and stall them
And see if they'll wait,
And say you feel real bad,
And you're sorry you're late.
But when they just keep
Adding to the pressure and pain,
Just weather the storm,
And when it rains, let it rain.
And at least be thankful that your
Gas gauge still works.
And that your phone's still connected,
Although when it rings it hurts.
And if it just hadn't been
For that bad check that you took,
You could pay all your bills
And get off the ol' hook.
But if you want to be sure,
You're paid for your work,
Get cash in advance from
All those deadbeat jerks!

I'LL JUST MAIL IT

I'll just mail it, it's easy that way.
You don't have to worry, you know I'll pay.
But my mail just came, and there's nothin' today.
So I guess I'll call 'em, and see what they say.
"Now... what's the amount you say is due?
Well, I don't know why, it wasn't sent to you.
You know us, we always pay on time,
And especially to you,
You being a friend of mine.
Do you have a copy of that bill?
If you make one for me, I promise I will
Mail it tomorrow, straight off to you,
'Cause I know you're anxious,
To be paid what's due.
We've been so busy of late you know,
We haven't had time to send you your dough.
But I'm glad you called, it's good talking to you.
You'll have it tomorrow, or... in a day or two."
Hello, oh hi, yeah, I know I'm late,
But the people who owe me are makin' me wait,
Yeah, I just talked to 'em,
And they said they'd pay,
Maybe tomorrow, but not today.
Ok, as soon as I get it, I'll mail it to you.
I'll do the best I can, that's all I can do.

FROM CAROLINE TO CALIFORNIA

From Caroline to California
I spend my time gripping this wheel,
But for me it's not as easy
As it was for Sonny and Will.
I spend my life meeting deadlines
To pull into the dock on time.
And I'm dang lucky if I can do it
Without paying many fines.
From Caroline to California,
I roll along from town to town.
Then when I get to where I'm going,
I've just got time to turn around.

RANDY

Randy drove that big truck
From sun to setting sun.
And he went through all those gears
And he never missed a one.
Eastbound or westbound
It made no difference to that boy
'Cause he handled that big truck
Just like it was a little toy.
Now the loads that he hauled,
He had to get them there just right.
Sometimes it was in the morning,
Sometimes it was late at night.
And yes, it was his job
To take good care of the load,
So rest and sleep was just something
That he grabbed along the road.
And to him it made no difference
As to what the weather might prove to be.
Sometimes it might be clear
Other times impossible to see.
And at 60 miles an hour
With 40 tons going down the road,
To some "KW" may mean Kenworth,
But to Randy it means "King of the Woad."

TO DAN AND JUANITA

Dan and Juanita, some friends of mine,
Like cowboy poetry, and from time to time,
Listen to some of the things that I write.
So, I wrote a few lines down for them tonight.

Dan and I've talked about a way of life,
And a feeling inside, that cuts like a knife,
It doesn't really matter at all what you do,
It's just a feeling inside,
That puts the cowboy in you.

Sometimes you can't tell just by lookin' at faces,
But there's cowboys and girls,
In all kinds of places.
To some it's a dream, to others it's more real.
But, to most it's a state of mind,
Or just how you feel.

Sometimes it's just a way of dealing with life,
Knowing how to handle little pleasures or strife.
Or, just knowing something
About things that grow,
And enjoying the rain or the new fallen snow.

Being a cowboy's not just a part time thing,
And it's more than just knowing,
What song to sing.

A cowboy's deep rooted
In his beliefs and ways,
And lives by his code on good or bad days.

To be a top hand, at whatever you do,
You've got to finish what you start,
It's called follow through.
So, if you wear faded jeans,
Or even a business suit,
Don't forget your hat and leave on those boots.

NEVER TOO OLD

"I doubt if I'll ever marry again"
He said to me, as I sat there with him.
"I had a wife and family before,
But that was then, it ain't no more.
We had a house with a garden out back.
I had a good job and all of that.
We leased some land and ran some cattle.
We were as they say, 'sittin' tall in the saddle',
And we had enough money to get us by,
But she said, 'so long, adios, goodbye,
I want to be on my own, see what I can do,
And I'm tired of being married to you.
A cowboy's wife, I don't want to be
I'm going to the city... don't follow me'.
Well, she remarried and began a new life.
But I've not been able to find a new wife.
Oh, I've had my girl friends, that is true,
But I've never again, said, 'I do'.
But don't feel sorry for me, my son,
I just haven't been able to find the right one."
Then when he finished talking,
And his story was told,
He said, "but I'll never give up,
'Cause you're never too old!"

WE'D LIKE TO HAVE
SOMEONE LIKE YOU, BUT...

"We need someone with experience"
It seems that's all I'd ever hear,
Back in the days when I was young,
Tryin' to start my life long career.
"We'd like to have someone just like you,
But who's done this kind o' work before.
And if it weren't for just that alone,
You'd be exactly what we're lookin' for."
Well, phrases like that sure do get old,
When you're out there trying to get hired.
And just pokin' around looking for work
Can make a fella plenty tired.
But usually something comes along
To start you on your way.
And you're eager to jump right in,
And do the job,
Although it's only for minimum pay.
Then you work real hard,
To show 'em you're good.
And when they put you to the test,
You show 'em exactly what you're worth,
And prove you can ride with the best.
Then comes a time down the road
When something might come along,
And somebody might say

"You can always work for me
If you ever think of movin' on."
But at that time, things are pretty flush,
And you wouldn't think of changing brands,
So you thank 'em kindly for thinkin' of you,
And decline and just shake hands.
Then without warning and from out of the blue,
The big boss sells the ranch.
And the next thing you know,
You're out lookin' again,
But at least now you've got a chance,
'Cause you've gotten to be known,
For what you can do,
And are called by most a top hand.
So it shouldn't be hard to ride in some yard
And get hired on with another brand.
So with the experience you've got,
You give it a thought,
And remember that offer before
"You can always work for me if ya ever think
Of movin' on."
So you ride out there and knock on their door.
"Well, we'd really like to have someone like you
But we're full up and aren't hiring right now.
But you won't have trouble finding some work,
you being so good at punchin' a cow."
Now although not discouraged,
You kind of worry,

Cause you remember that time back when
You first started out lookin' for work,
And how things had been kind of slim.
But that was then when you were green
And besides, you've got "experience" now.
And you can do any job, what ever it is
Be it fixin' fence or punchin' a cow.
The only trouble now wherever you go
You hear another excuse in reply.
"We'd like to have someone like you,
But you're over qualified!"

ON PARENTS AND CHILDREN

That children are not miniature adults,
And must do more than merely grow,
Is an important fact that both the children
And the parents must know.
It's important that the ones who are in charge
And the ones who are in control,
Are the parents, not the children,
And that both have an important role.
Children must be taught, in order to learn,
And their only rights,
Are the ones which they earn.
A time for play, for meals, and for bed,
A time to bathe, to learn, and to do what is said.
Discipline is important for kids as they grow,
They must learn that "yes" means yes,
And that "no" means no.
Responsibilities with rewards at the end,
That should not be bribes,
But should be something to win,
For accomplishments well done, again and again.
Manners and respect, more lessons to be taught
By the parents of the children,
And it seems like a lot,
But they're little and young for just a short time,
So, say it with pride when you say,
"That kid is mine!"

AN IDAHO SPUD

He said, "I'll take a potato, a russet,
You know, an Idaho Spud.
And I'd like you to bake it for me,
Please, if you would.
Don't wrap it in foil or cut it with a knife,
Bake it like I tell you,
If you treasure your life.
Just stick it in the oven at about 400 degrees hot.
If you don't cook it like that,
You might as well let it rot.
Now for about an hour, you can let it bake,
And if you do like I say,
You can't make a mistake.
Then blossom it nicely when you serve it to me.
Just poke it with a fork, like this here... see?
Then push on each end, so it can fluff right up.
And... you better bake two.
One might not be enough!"

"NICE FOLKS"

Oh, I'd danced before, but had always ignored
Any kind of formal instruction.
I'd always assumed that if I felt the beat,
It would reach my feet
But it was a right poor assumption.
Then I was asked one night,
By a girlfriend of mine
If I'd take her to this class.
Well, I balked at first,
But thought things could get worse
At the thought of not getting any... dinner.
I didn't know my left from my right
When I first walked into that hall.
But it didn't take long to learn that night,
Except, when I faced a new wall!
"Well, that's ok" I heard him say,
When I was in this big old line.
"To learn this dance,
You've got to learn each wall,
And I'll teach 'em to you, one at a time."
Now as time went by, I did learn some steps,
No matter what the wall.
And I met a lot of folks, and made new friends,
And looked forward to goin' to the hall.
Now there's hundreds of people
He's taught to dance,
In a country and western way.

And he's helped country dancing,
Become what it is,
On the coast near the Monterey Bay.
And like most he taught, I became a friend
And really hated to see him go.
But there was a big demand to learn to dance
By the people in Ohio.
So he bought a new place and headed East,
And it was sad to see him leave,
But I guess we can't keep him all to ourselves
And there's really no need to grieve.
'Cause with his wife by his side,
And a tear in his eye,
He said with his hat o'er his heart,
"I'll always be best friends with each of you,
No matter how many miles we're apart.
And if you ever get the chance to come out East,
And want to dance like we've done before,
You're always welcome to stay with us,
'Cause we've always got plenty of floor."
So to say "nice folks", why, it just ain't enough
When lookin' for a way to describe
These folks I know, that taught me to dance,
And when I say,
"I know 'em", I say it with pride!

51   *Remuda Dust*

MIKE AND CAREN

He came out to the West Coast,
From back in Ohio.
What he'd find in California,
He didn't really know.
But he loaded what was his,
And made the trip out West,
He'd give it what he had, and try to do his best.
Now a gal from Minnesota, who had left that
State behind,
Also came to California,
Not knowin' what she'd find.
And they met up with each other,
As you probably have guessed.
But this story ain't quite over,
So let me tell you 'bout the rest.
Well, they got sweet on one another,
Of that there is no doubt.
They planned a little wedding,
And sent some invites out,
To all their friends and families,
Like you always do,
So they can be there with you when you say,
"I do".
And in the Golden State of California,
You know... the promised land,
They made a promise to each other with a little
Golden band.

53   *Remuda Dust*

THE CAMPING TRIP

She said,
"Let's go camping in the middle of the week,
Take three or four days and get away.
Let's go up to the mountains,
Near a lake or a creek,
Just fish and swim and lay around all day."

She said we'd just take a few simple things,
Since we wouldn't be gone all that long.
But, by the time I got the truck all loaded up,
She admitted that she might have been wrong.

We took our sleeping bags and fishing poles,
And a chest that held three blocks of ice.
And all kinds of clothes for hot or for cold,
And a porta-pottie, cause she thought it'd be nice.

We took pots and pans, and other camping gear,
And all sorts of things to survive.
I think we wound up taking,
Everything we'd ever bought,
Since the very first day we'd been alive.

She said, "Let's take the dog,
'Cause he can guard our camp,
When we're asleep and in our tent at night.

But, I don't think she figured,
That if he met a skunk,
He'd be smart enough to not pick a fight.

Well, we got out on the road,
And were finally on our way,
We just could not have picked a better day.
But, then along about noon, the sky clouded up,
And things started looking kind of gray.

We thought we'd better stop,
And cover up our load,
'Cause we didn't want all that gear gettin' wet.
So, we dug out the tarp,
From the bottom of the truck,
But, when we tried to reload,
Nothing seemed to fit.

And when we got things covered,
And back in the truck,
We'd both gotten soakin' wet.
But, if you want to see what happens by the end
Of this story,
You'll find that we hadn't seen nothing yet.

When we got to our campsite,
It was really coming down,
And we had to build a shelter for our tent.

And we decided that if we knew all this was
Going to happen,
We'd a stayed home and would never have went.

But there we were in our camp,
300 miles from home,
Thinkin' this bad weather just can't last.
So, we just sat there and weathered the storm,
And as it turns out,
We'd both been right, when considering
The length of the storm.
'Cause on the day we left, the storm had passed
And the weather was turnin' kind o' warm.

And one night when we were out there, just
Sitting by the fire,
We roasted something that we couldn't eat.
Our shoes started smokin',
And the flames went higher
While trying to warm and dry our feet.

Well, we did a little hiking,
And a little bit of fishing,
And swam in the lake made of melted snow.
And ate bacon and potatoes,
That we cooked on the fire,
And when we left we really didn't want to go.

We packed up our camp,
And headed down the mountain,
Taking time to enjoy all the scenery.
Little did we know, that time was what we had,
And we had plenty of it facing her and me.

Well, after about 12 miles of mountain dirt road,
We hit the two lane black top towards home.
Then we heard this funny noise,
And smelled something burning.
It seems our alternator took a hike and was gone.

But, as luck would have it,
Not too far down the road,
Was this sign that read "complete auto repair".
And out stepped this man smiling ear to ear,
And said,
"How can I help", as he combed his hair.

He said, "I can help you",
When I told him what was wrong.
He said, "I can fix it quick,
And have you on your way.
The only problem is, the part that you need,
I just don't happen to have in stock today."

He said, "Now you know this is Saturday,
And we all close early,
So, it looks like you're just gonna have to stay.

But, there's a place across the street,
That'll rent you a room,
So you'll have a place until Monday."

Well I think I met the guy we all hear about,
Whenever we hear a story like this.
He'll make you stay and make you wait and try
To take your money,
And claims it's just the nature of his business.

We stayed across the street, in the only hotel,
That there was for 20 miles around,
We stayed there until that next Monday,
Until the part that we needed could be found.

They fed us real good,
And sympathized with our miseries,
And told us all about the folks in town.
Then they loaned us their truck,
To go get the replacement
For that part that had broken down.

Well, I drove 100 miles to get that precious part,
And the first thing I noticed on that shop door,
Was their sign that said "We're open every day,
Including Saturday, until at least four."

When I found out I could have,
Been there on Saturday,
It made the hair on my neck stand on end.
And if that dude with the well groomed hair,
Had been there beside me,
Well, I think I might have murdered him.

So I got back on the road,
With that brand new part,
And drove 100 miles the other way.
But, when I got back to where my truck was
Broken down,
They said,
"You might have to wait another day."

"We got an emergency call for another tow,
And we're headin' out to pick 'em up right now.
We can't spend the time on a little job like yours,
I'm sure you all can fix it yourself, somehow."

Then, the girl who worked at the place we stayed
Said, "You know my husband works on cars
From time to time,
And he's off work today.
I'll get him down here to help you,
He'll fix your truck and,
Won't charge you a dime."

Then I thought to myself,
Where had this guy been?
Since the very first day we limped into town.
I could have gone for that part two days ago,
When that pickup truck of mine first broke down.

Well, he put that part in, in less than 10 minutes,
We thanked him and said, "We'll see you later."
And I think that when I go camping again,
The next time I'll take along a spare alternator!

"COOKIE"

He packs for our camp the supplies we need.
He's the first one to get there,
And the last one to leave.
To keep the salt, sugar, coffee and flour dry,
He puts 'em in the wagon,
And stacks 'em up high.
The knives, pots and pans and tubs that he takes
Hang on the back or sides
Of the wagon someplace.
And when the weather's fair and there's no
Chance of rain,
He'll pull back the tarp and air out everything.
Now you don't want to criticize
Him all that much,
'Less you want something to eat with his own
Special touch.
'Cause if you complain too much,
About what's to eat,
The next time it's prairie chicken and biscuits,
You just might get biscuits and feet.
But biscuits and feet aren't really all that bad,
When compared to some of the main courses
We've had.
Like ground hog pie, or coyote stew,
Or road-kill squirrel in its' own gravy for you.
Or a cactus sandwich, that's a real trick to eat.
But if you're good enough at it,

At the same time you chew,
You can pick your teeth.
And sometimes it takes a whole lot of nerve
Just to look, let alone eat,
At some things that he'll serve.
Most times he's called "Cookie", but he's got
Other names too,
Depending on what he's cooking,
For me and for you.

MUSTANG ROUND UP

"Head 'em off boys, they're comin' yer way!
Try and turn 'em around!" We heard 'em say.
We weren't on drag, we's ridin' wide,
Kinda driftin' along, a little sleepy eyed,
When we heard the boys who'd been eatin' dust,
Yellin' and screamin' and hollerin' at us.
"Get 'em turned boys, and slow 'em down'
'For they run 'emselves half way to town!"
Well, we spurred up quick,
Sittin' deep in the saddle,
An' built us our loops, like for hazin' cattle.
But these were mustangs we's bringin' in,
That'd caught a whiff,
O' somethin' strange in the wind.
And what ever it was that had made 'em bolt,
Made 'em all as spooky as a two-year old colt.
So we raced like hell to cut off the lead horse,
But, failed to notice this ditch... and of course,
Were promptly separated from our mounts,
And quickly went down,
And were out for the count.
Now, when the boys got 'em turned,
And finally slowed down,
We was just pickin' ourselves up off the ground.
We were all covered in a mud of sweat and dirt,
But, what the heck, we's okay,
And we didn't get hurt.

65   *Remuda Dust*

THE BIG BOSS

The Big Boss has a special job for me,
And tho' I consider myself to be a top hand,
There's been lots of times,
When I don't understand.
Why pick on me?
Why, sometimes it don't seem fair,
'Cause I've done plenty of the dirty work,
Can't they send somebody else out there?
There's lots of others who can do the job,
Why can't he call Ernie or Joe,
Or Charlie or Bob?
And, if it's always me who gets the call,
'Cause I just happen to be tougher than most,
Why am I eatin' beans and not a fat juicy roast?
Well, I'll do the job, now don't get me wrong,
But sometimes it's dang hard,
To stay up and hang on.
Now I try and sit 'em salty,
And sit deep in the saddle,
But there's times when I actually think
I can hear my brain rattle.
And sometimes a rank horse can be so tough,
That I want to say,
"I quit, now, I've had enough!"
So, when I need extra help, as I often do,
I call on the Big Boss himself,
To help pull me through.

And whatever the task,
Or whatever the ride,
I can count on him being there by my side.
And from the power there is in a little prayer,
I know that the Big Boss will always be there.

HELLO, THE CAMP!

"Hello, the camp!", came the call,
By a man in a saddle, sittin' straight and tall.
"I'm comin' on in, don't be alarmed.
I'm comin' in peaceful, an' I'm unarmed.
I spotted your fire from a top the hill,
And I'm kinda tired an' hungry,
Could you spare a meal?"
The night was lit by a hunter's moon,
And a man with a guitar,
Strummed a lonesome tune.
The cattle were restin' and all bedded down,
And they were miles and miles,
From any real town.
They let into the camp,
This man in the saddle,
The cowboys in charge of this herd of cattle.
"Where are you from and where are you goin'?"
The trail boss asked some things,
That needed knowin'.
"I'm from the 5 Bar E and have horses for sale,
And I've been about ten days now,
Out on the trail.
My horses are grazin',
A couple of miles from here,
They're all good stock, and can run like a deer.

I'm headed to the fort,
'Cause I hear the Army's buyin',
Accordin' to this here notice I've got...
I hope it ain't lying.
But I'm short on supplies and lookin' to trade,
Would you all be interested in a few head...
All top grade.
I don't need much to finish my trip,
And if you're interested in tradin',
I'll give you your pick."
As he had some chuck and sat by the fire,
We wondered if he was an honest man,
Or was he a liar.
The trail boss said, "Our supplies,
Are a little short too,
And we might not have enough,
If we traded with you."
He said he understood,
He knew times were tough,
And that he'd be on his way,
And thanks for the chuck.
Then we called the extra guard out,
For the night, and those that got to sleep,
Just slept kind o' light.

The moon got real big before
Slippin' off the edge.
And the man with the guitar had gone off to bed.
The cattle were content for the rest of the night,
And he who yelled "Hello, the camp!",
Rode out into the night.

OUR COMMUNITY

Just a few short miles from town,
Where they still plant and
Grow things in the ground,
You'll find a little country store.
There's a dentist and post office too,
A friendly church for me and you,
A firehouse, a ladies club, and a little bit more,
There's a triangular shaped piece of ground,
At this place that's just out of town,
And a ball field at the school not far away,
There's a rock monument
With some grass around,
And a big tall pole sticking in the ground,
Where the flag is raised and lowered every day.
There's always a stray dog or two,
Just waitin' to share your lunch with you,
'Cause there's always someone there
To give 'em a bite.
And the little store about which we speak,
Stays open seven days a week,
But closes by six o'clock each and every night.
You can report a fire or mail a card.
The ladies club meets in their own backyard.
And, you can pray, or drill and fill a cavity.
You can buy a beer or a sandwich to go,
And everyone you see will say hello.
That's the way it is in our community.

FALLIN' ASLEEP

Late in the evenin', when the sun's gone down,
And I'm in my blankets,
I've spread on the ground,
My mind starts driftin',
While lookin' up at the sky,
And thoughts cross my mind,
That make me wonder why.
I lay there and ponder, the spectacular show,
That I see in the sky, as my fire burns low.
The scent from my fire of sage and mesquite,
Adds to the comfort of the night,
As I rest my feet.
The sky's all around me, and touches the ground,
And the quiet of the night,
Gives way to the sound,
Of the night livin' creatures that hide by day,
But now surround me, out here where I lay.
My horse sighs with content,
As I listen to him feed,
While he munches on grass that's full of seed.
From a crackling spark that pops from the fire,
A thin column of smoke makes a wavy spire.
As it reaches upward, and slowly flies,
I drift off with it, and close my eyes.

73   *Remuda Dust*

THE

END

75   *Remuda Dust*